A LETTER TO AMY

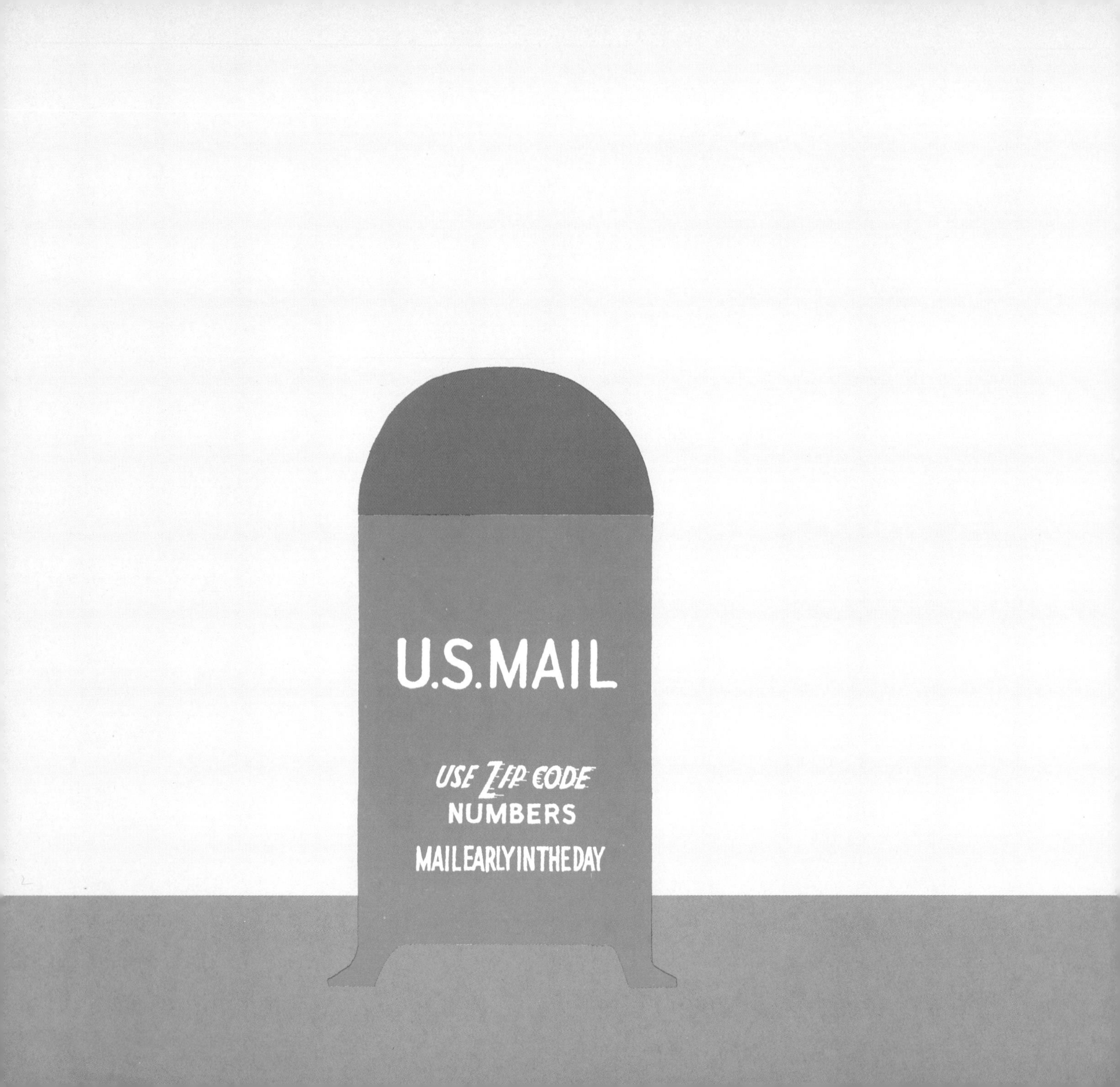
U.S. MAIL
USE ZIP CODE
NUMBERS
MAIL EARLY IN THE DAY

EZRA JACK KEATS

A LETTER TO AMY

PUFFIN BOOKS

"I'm writing a letter to Amy.
I'm inviting her to my party," Peter announced.
"Why don't you just ask her? You didn't write
to anyone else," said his mother.
Peter stared at the sheet of paper for a while and said,
"We-e-el-l, this way it's sort of special."

He folded the letter quite a few times,
put it in the envelope, and sealed it.
"Now I'll mail it," he said.
"What did you write?" his mother asked.
WILL YOU PLEASE COME
TO MY BIRTHDAY PARTY. PETER.
"You should tell her when to come."
So he wrote on the back of the envelope:
IT IS THIS SATURDAY AT 2.
"Now I'll mail it."
"Put on a stamp."
He did, and started to leave.
"Wear your raincoat. It looks like rain."
He put it on and said, "It looks like rain.
You'd better stay in, Willie,"
and ran out to mail his letter.

Walking to the mailbox, Peter looked at the sky.
Dark clouds raced across it like wild horses.
He glanced up at Amy's window. She wasn't there.
Only Pepe, her parrot, sat peering down.
"Willie! Didn't I tell you to stay home?"

It is this Saturday at 2.

Peter thought, What will the boys say
when they see a girl at my party?
Suddenly there was a flash of lightning
and a roar of thunder!
A strong wind blew the letter out of his hand!

Peter chased the letter.
He tried to stop it with his foot, but it blew away.

Then it flew high into the air—

and landed, skipping across a hopscotch game.

The letter blew this way and that.
Peter chased it this way and that.
He couldn't catch it.

Big drops of rain began to fall.
Just then someone turned the corner.
It was Amy! She waved to him.
The letter flew right toward her.

She mustn't see it, or the surprise will be spoiled!
They both ran for the letter.

In his great hurry, Peter bumped into Amy.
He caught the letter before she could see it was for her.

Quickly he stuffed the letter into the mailbox.
He looked for Amy, but she had run off crying.

Now she'll never come to my party, thought Peter.
He saw his reflection in the street.
It looked all mixed up.

When Peter got back to his house, his mother asked, "Did you mail your letter?"
"Yes," he said sadly.

Saturday came at last.
Everybody arrived but Amy.

"Shall I bring the cake out now?" his mother asked Peter.
"Let's wait a little," said Peter.
"Now! Bring it out now!" chanted the boys.
"All right," said Peter slowly, "bring it out now."

Just then the door opened.
In walked Amy with her parrot!
"A girl—ugh!" said Eddie.

"Happy Birthday, Peter!" said Amy.
"HAAPPY BIRRRTHDAY, PEEETERRR!"
repeated the parrot.

Peter's mother brought in the cake she had baked and lit the candles. Everyone sang.

"Make a wish!" cried Amy.

"Wish for a truck full of ice cream!" shouted Eddie.

"A store full of candy and no stomach-ache!"

But Peter made his own wish,
and blew out all the candles at once.

PUFFIN BOOKS
Published by the Penguin Group
Penguin Putnam Books for Young Readers, 345 Hudson Street,
New York, New York 10014, U.S.A.
Penguin Books Ltd, 27 Wrights Lane, London W8 5TZ, England
Penguin Books Australia Ltd, Ringwood, Victoria, Australia
Penguin Books Canada Ltd, 10 Alcorn Avenue, Toronto, Ontario, Canada M4V 3B2
Penguin Books (N.Z.) Ltd, 182-190 Wairau Road, Auckland 10, New Zealand

Penguin Books Ltd, Registered Offices: Harmondsworth, Middlesex, England

First published in the United States of America by Harper & Row Publishers, 1968

Published by Viking and Puffin Books, members of Penguin Putnam Books for Young Readers, 1998

33 34 35 36 37 38 39 40

Copyright © Ezra Jack Keats, 1968
All rights reserved

LIBRARY OF CONGRESS CATALOGING-IN-PUBLICATION DATA
Keats, Ezra Jack.
A letter to Amy / Ezra Jack Keats.
p. cm.
Summary: Peter wants to invite Amy to his birthday party but he
wants it to be a surprise.
ISBN 978-0-670-88063-8. —ISBN 978-0-14-056442-6 (pbk.)
[1. Birthdays—Fiction.] I. Title.
PZ7.K2253Le 1998 [E]—dc21 97-49433 CIP AC

Manufactured in China